What is Black Lives Matter?

a story for kids

by Salina Harris

What is Black Lives Matter?

a story for kids

by Salina Harris

illustrations by J. L. Stovall

Noah's coming over to play. Hooray!
I planned cool things for us to do today.

We can ride bikes and even build tents.
Collect rocks, read books, and play instruments.

After snack time, I got anxious and bored.
Mommy said, “While waiting for Noah,
be sure you finish your chores.”

Before long the doorbell rang and what did I see?
My best friend Noah in front of me.

Noah and I are just like brothers.
Two peas in a pod like no other.

We played and had fun while my parents talked.
Then they took us out for a nice, long walk.

After Noah left, mommy started tidying and cleaning. Daddy turned on the news. There were lots of people on TV.

They were shouting, holding signs, and marching the streets.
I must admit, that it frightened me.

There were grown-ups and big kids and lots of police.
I wanted to know, what did all of this mean?

Daddy noticed that I looked very scared.
And then he gave me a tight hug to show that he cared.

"What's wrong, Josh? Why do you seem so blue?
Tell Daddy all that is bothering you."

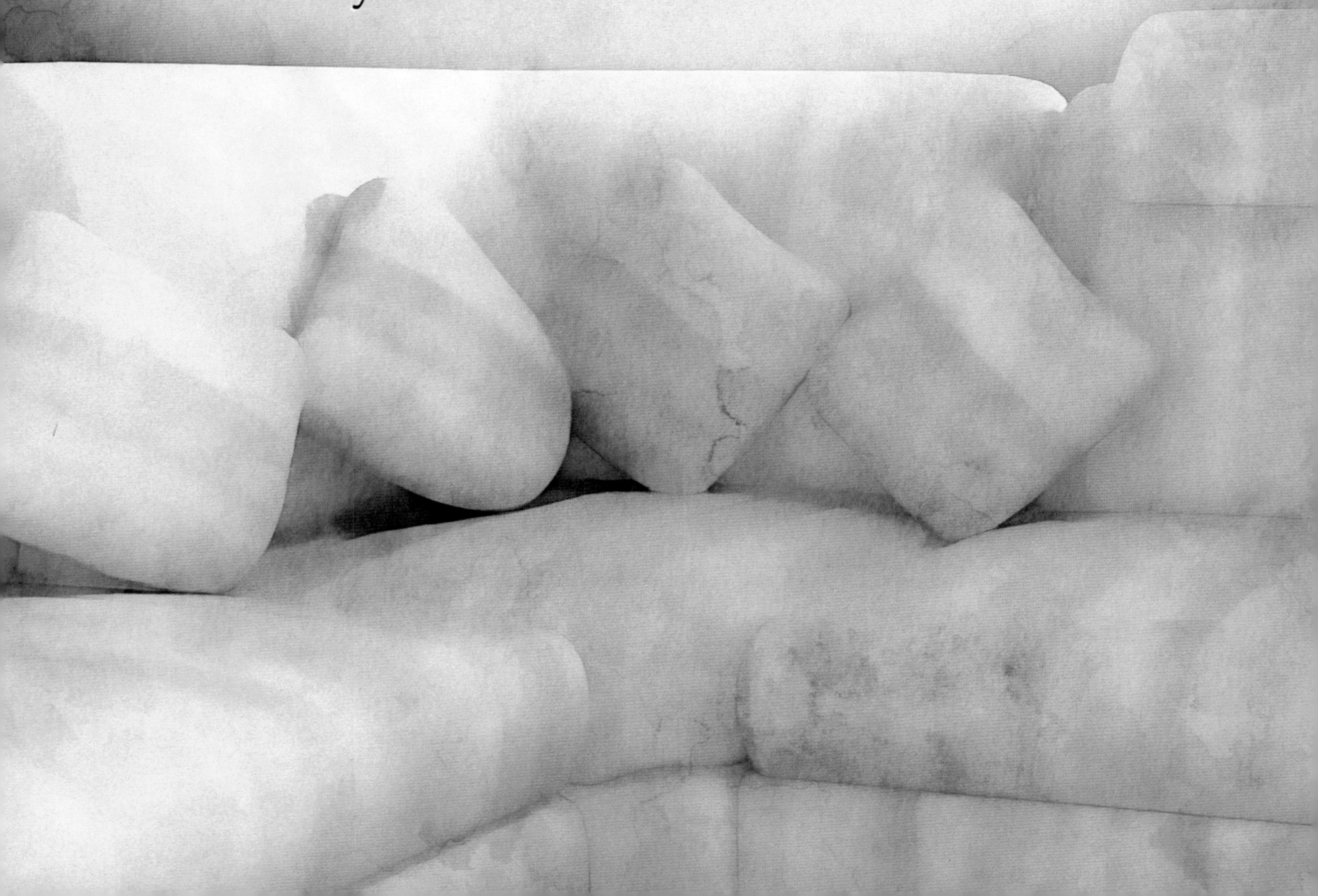

With a look of concern, I pointed to the news.
I let him know that's what was making me blue.

"Daddy, what are they doing on the TV?
Can you explain what is going on, please?"

Then mommy chimed in, that there's been
lots of chatter.
And it's all about a movement called,
Black Lives Matter.

"Some people don't like others because of the
color of their skin,
Instead of seeing all of the beauty that lies within."

“Well Noah is white, and I am black,
And we don’t treat each other like that.”

“That’s because you’re true friends,
no matter your race.
If the world thought like you two,
it would be a much better place.”

“So no matter what baby, make sure
as you grow,
You do not judge others, wherever you go.”

I nodded and then made a promise to be,
The person who loves others, beyond what I see.

Together we're like a rainbow, all shades and colors.
But although we are different, we should
respect one another.

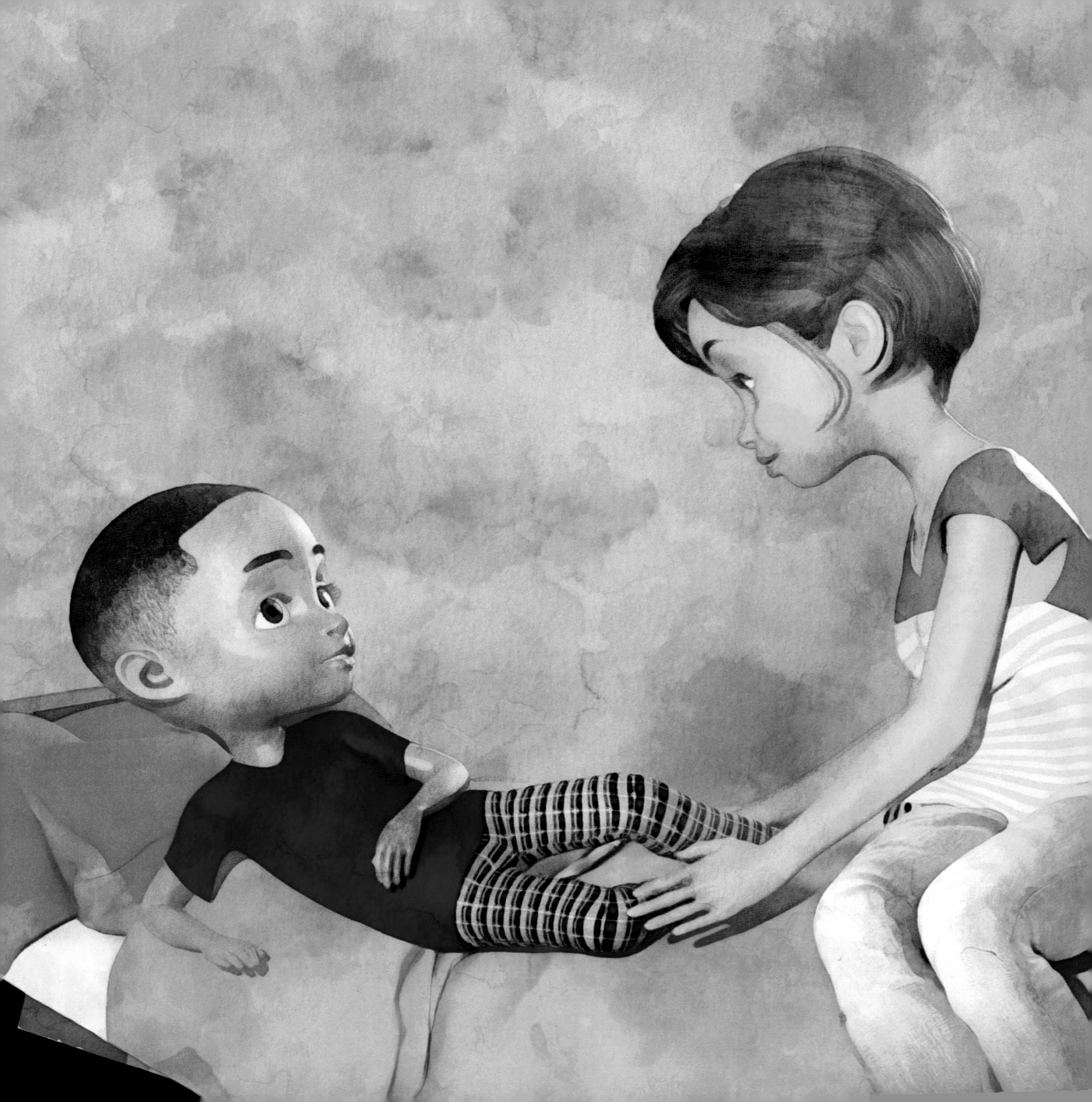

And before bedtime, when Mommy and Daddy
gave me a kiss.
I closed my eyes tight and made one special wish.

That one day our skin color won't have to matter.

And all the world will truly believe that all lives matter.

Made in the USA
Monee, IL
24 June 2021

72203214R00019